The Case
of the
Stolen
Stallion

D1457935

By Jesse Leon McCann

SCHOLASTIC INC.

New York   Toronto   London   Auckland   Sydney
Mexico City   New Delhi   Hong Kong

ISBN 0-439-20655-3

Lyrics to Ace's theme song by Ron Alaveda.

Copyright © 2000 by Morgan Creek Productions, Inc.
All rights reserved.
Published by Scholastic Inc.
Scholastic and associated logos are trademarks and/or registered trademarks of Scholastic Inc.
Designed by Keirsten Geise

12 11 10 9 8 7 6 5 4 3 2 1   0 1 2 3 4 5 6/0

Printed in the U.S.A.

First Scholastic printing, November 2000

Ace's Theme Song

Ace Ventura, Pet Detective
Alrighty then!
He can sniff like a dog
He's slippery as a frog
Ace Ventura!
Radar like a bat
He's a way cool cat
That's Ace
If there's a tail
He's on the trail
He's sooo protective!
Even if his brain seems defective
Ace Ventura, Pet Detective
He can roar back in time
'N' save a dino in distress
Ace Ventura
He'll squash an alien bug
Eeeeuuuuw . . .
What a mess!
Ooooo, Ace!
He's pesky as a flea
Stings like a bee
Swings like a monkey and . . .
. . . Oooo what a hunk . . .
He's Ace Ventura, Pet Detective
Ace Ventura!
Alrighty then!

"Alrighty then!" Ace Ventura, the world's greatest — and *only* — pet detective, exclaimed. "Hi-ho Humphrey, away!"

With that, Humphrey — Ace's racing camel — took off like a shot!

Spike the wonder monkey, Ace's semi-faithful simian sidekick, had been sitting on Humphrey's back, relaxing, enjoying the sights, and munching on delicious figs. He didn't realize the race was about to start. When it did, he fell off backward, head over paws.

Now Spike was hanging onto Humphrey's tail, running behind the camel across the hot, *hot* sand.

"Ook, eek eek!" Spike screeched, only Ace didn't hear him.

One hundred camels dashed across the Saudi Arabian desert. Dust flew from their mighty hooves. They galloped faster and faster.

Ace and Spike had come to the Middle Eastern country of Saudi Arabia to enter the race. You had to pay to participate, and the money raised went to one of Ace's favorite charities. Have you ever smelled a camel's breath? *Hooo-wheee!* You *don't* want to go there!

"This is all for a very worthy cause, and I just love a challenge!" Ace yelled over the noise. "Don't you agree, Spike? The thrill of victory . . ."

The agony of da feet! thought Spike. He leaped off the scalding hot sand and onto Humphrey's back. But because of the way camels are built, Spike had a hard time holding on.

Ace reached behind him and grabbed Spike. Then he used his monkey to wipe the dust off his racing goggles.

"Oog!" Spike said angrily. He hated it when Ace did that! But he was glad when Ace placed him snugly in the saddle.

Ace, Spike, and Humphrey took an

early lead. They left most of the pack in the dust. Ace knew animals better than almost anyone. Okay, *better* than *everyone*! And he knew that Humphrey would race better to *music* than to being bopped on the fanny with a long stick. That's what the other racers were doing. Ace sang to Humphrey instead, and used a penny whistle to play him tunes.

"This is K.A.M.L., all camel music, all the time," Ace said in a radio deejay voice. "Here's one of my favorite oldies. I'm sure it's one of yours!"

Ace started singing to Humphrey, *"Oh, we got the hump, gotta have that hump!"* and then played the penny whistle, *"Tweet-tweet!"*

Humphrey immediately picked up speed.

"See, Spike?" Ace observed proudly. "To win a race, sing to your animal. Of course, it helps to have a *super* singing voice, like me!"

Spike rolled his eyes and shook his head. *Yeah, whatever.*

The racers were heading toward tall sand dunes, far above a winding river. A sturdy wood-and-rope bridge spanned the river. A few hundred yards on the other side of the bridge was the finish line.

Ace looked back at the other racers. "Well, I guess we all know who's the top camel jockey in these here parts!" he chortled. "Loooosers!"

Then Ace's eyes flew wide open. Surprise! A huge camel was barreling down on them. The rider grinned evilly as he spurred his great beast forward.

The man on the camel was big, mean Eyepatch Pete. He got the nickname "Eyepatch" because he wore one over his left eye, like a pirate.

Eyepatch Pete caught up to Ace. They raced side by side. Eyepatch was whipping his camel with a stick to make him go as fast as he could. The camel looked really sad.

Ace had an idea. He grabbed Eyepatch's stick away from him.

"You know, you could put somebody's eye out with this thing!" Ace advised. "In fact, maybe you already did!" Then Ace whipped Eyepatch on his bottom with the stick. *Whack!*

"Ow!" cried Eyepatch.

"Funny, it didn't seem that painful when you were doing it to your camel," Ace noted.

Eyepatch Pete growled and pulled the reins. His camel veered right into Humphrey's path. *BAM!*

Eyepatch bumped them on purpose. Hard. The bigger camel passed by and raced onto the bridge. Humphrey, with Ace and Spike aboard, wobbled, stumbled, *and missed the bridge.*

Humphrey, Ace, and Spike were heading right over the edge of the cliff!

Humphrey shuffled and staggered on the brink. But at the last minute, he stopped short, right on the edge.

Whew! Ace and Spike breathed a sigh of relief.

Then the dirt under Humphrey's hooves crumbled, and he started toppling into the gorge!

Quickly, Humphrey reached out with his teeth and clamped down on one of the bridge's ropes. Luckily, camels have very strong teeth! As Ace and Spike hung onto the rope for dear life, Humphrey swung across the gorge like an ape swinging on a vine in the jungle. In fact, they swung all the way to the other side of the gorge — just where they wanted to be!

"Gravy! This must be what Tarzan feels like!" Ace cried happily. He let loose with a jungle yell. "Aaaaah-ayah!"

On the other side of the bridge was the

finish line. A crowd had gathered to watch the race end, and they cheered as Ace, Spike, and Humphrey swung toward them.

Eyepatch couldn't believe what he was seeing. His camel was so surprised, he stopped in his tracks. Eyepatch Pete flew off his back and kept going. He landed headfirst in a big jar.

Meanwhile, Humphrey hopped over the finish line — right into the winner's circle.

"Thank you! Thank you!" Ace said as he was handed a big trophy. "It's a great honor. I'd like to thank — one at a time — every animal I've ever known."

Spike covered his eyes. Oh no! This was going to take *forever!*

"First, Aaron, the aardvark . . ."

But Ace never got to continue his speech. For, out of nowhere, a big limousine pulled up. Two huge men got out, grabbed Ace and Spike, threw them into the back of the car, and drove off in a swirl of dust.

Ace and Spike had been kidnapped!

Chapter 3

Half an hour later, the limousine pulled up at a grand palace. It was near an oasis in the desert.

Ace and Spike were hustled into a big room. There, a stern, elegant man sat on a throne. He was dressed in fine, colorful silks, and wore a turban.

"Do you know who I am?" the man demanded.

"Why, of course." Ace smiled. "You're that magician who does the midnight show in Las Vegas."

The man and his servants looked at one another.

"Let's see how good you *really* are! How much change do I have in my pocket?" Ace asked.

"No, Mr. Ventura," said the man. "I am Sheik Baba-Ben-Louie. This is my palace."

"Kooky!" said Ace, heading toward the

door. "Although I don't know how *sheik* it is to steal people right in the middle of their victory party. Ta ta, now. Buh-*bye!*"

Spike didn't really want to leave. He had just noticed servants holding plates of nuts, dates, and other goodies. And he was hungry.

"Wait, Mr. Ventura!" Sheik Louie cried. "I have need of your services! My precious black stallion has been stolen!"

Ace stopped in his tracks. Helping animals was his mission in life. He turned back to Sheik Louie and cupped his hands on either side of his head. "I'm all ears."

All right! They were staying awhile! Spike happily dived at the goodies on the plates.

"My stallion's name is Starlight," Sheik Louie explained. "He was stolen by a most unusual thief."

Sheik Louie described how he had gotten up to ride Starlight that morning. But when he entered the royal stables, the strangest thing happened. Someone else was with the stallion. Sheik Louie had clicked on the lights to see who the intruder was.

He was shocked to see . . . it was *himself*! Or someone pretending to be him.

Sheik Louie's identical twin was sitting on Starlight's back. That was *really* weird, since he didn't have a twin. His double cackled and rode Starlight out of the stables. By the time Sheik Louie had roused his guards, the thief had disappeared into the desert with the horse.

"We tried to follow Starlight's tracks," Sheik Louie concluded. "But the wind blew them away."

Spike gobbled down handfuls of almonds. Listening to the sad story, a sudden feeling came over him. Was he feeling sorry for the sheik? No, that wasn't it.

Burp!

That was it!

"Won't you take my case, Mr. Ventura?" Sheik Louie pleaded. "I'll pay a fortune to get Starlight back."

Ace laughed. "Hah! Money? I laugh at such tokens when a member of the animal kingdom is in danger! I scoff at worldly possessions! For whenever a four-footed friend is in jeopardy, I'll be there! And whenever a furry *amigo* is lost, misplaced, or stolen, I'll also be there! It is the credo of the pet detective. Right, Spike?!"

Ace stopped short. Spike was looking at him like he was nuts.

"By the way, how *much* of a fortune?" Ace said sheepishly.

"I am prepared to pay you this much," Sheik Louie said, handing Ace a note.

"Ree-hee-hee-eally? Pardon me while I discuss the financials with my hairy little money manager," Ace said, passing the note to Spike.

"Awwk??" Spike went cross-eyed. Then he started jumping up and down and doing handsprings. He couldn't believe it.

Ace joined Spike in the victory dance. They did a *very* big dance. "Yes! Yes! Yes! Can you feel it, Spike?!"

Ace decided to start his search for the stolen stallion at the scene of the crime, the stables. Then he would track the thief through the desert.

"But how will you be able to find the thief in the vast desert?" Sheik Louie wondered.

"Worry not, my dear sheik!" Ace smiled. "Your twin troublemaker unwittingly left a trail. This!"

Ace held out his hand. In it was a pile of oats. Ace took a deep breath and rapidly explained:

"You feed Starlight some of the finest oats on earth." Ace put some in his mouth. "Yummy! Imported from County

Culberry, Ireland, if I'm not mistaken! The farmers of Culberry take pride in their oats's rich flavor, agreeable texture, and above all — *sniff!* — pleasant aroma!"

Spike snatched some of the oats out of Ace's hands. Mmmm! They *were* good.

"It appears the thief took several sacks of the oats with him," Ace continued. "One of the sacks seems to have sprung a leak, because I can smell oats in the desert — leading thataway!"

Ace pointed. Then he and Spike mounted Humphrey.

"Farewell, Sheik Baba-Ben-Louie! I'll return *with* your mighty stallion, or not at all!"

Spike watched Sheik Louie wave goodbye as they set out into the dangerous sands of the Rub' Al Khali desert. He wondered if they would ever return.

Chapter 4

Ace and Spike rode Humphrey deep into the desert. The trail of oats was easy to follow. The sun shone brightly.

Ace was cheerful. "Ah, the sun, the fresh air, the glory of Mother Nature at her finest!"

An hour later, Ace wasn't so cheerful. "Can't breathe, need water . . ." he choked as he swallowed the last of the water.

Another hour went by. The sun got hotter and hotter. Ace looked miserable. "If I *ever* meet Mother Nature, I'm gonna punch her right in the nose!" he said hoarsely. "Spike, my sweaty simian side-kick! If we don't find some shade soon . . . we're going to melt like an ice cube in a hot tub factory."

Spike had an idea — for himself any-way. He climbed under Humphrey and hung upside down from the saddle strap. *Ah! Shade!*

"Hey Spike! Look . . . what I . . . can do!" Ace dizzily put his finger to his lips and moved his lips back and forth. *"A-beeb! A-beeb! A-beeb! A-beeb!"*

The little monkey sighed. The heat was getting to Ace. He was starting to do even nuttier things than usual.

Then *Spike* started seeing things. Was the heat getting to him, too?

First, he saw mountains of ice cream instead of sand dunes. Then a line of swaying palm trees that turned into hula dancers. And then, right in front of them, Sheik Louie was floating in the air like a spirit. *Then* Louie transformed into their old enemy, Faust! Faust was an evil sorcerer who liked to collect and trade magical, unusual animals. Ace and Spike had defeated him many times in the past.

"Eeek-o-oop!" Spike screamed.

"Greetings, Ace Ventura and Spike!" The floating image spoke!

Humphrey was so frightened, he reared up, throwing Ace and Spike into the air. Then he bolted. Soon he was gone from sight.

"Interesting," Ace said. "This is the first time I've had a mirage *talk* to me."

Spike jumped up, surprised. *Ace could see the mirage, too?* "Ook! Eeeb, oop!" Spike chattered.

"What's that you say, Spike? You can also see Faust?" Ace exclaimed, coming to his senses. "Then that's no mirage! There's sorcery afoot!"

"That is correct, pet detective!" Faust's ghostlike image sneered. "I left this spirit message of myself behind. I knew you would be on the case. It was I who disguised myself as the sheik's twin and stole his magnificent stallion. But there's nothing you can do about it! Ha ha ha!"

"Yeah? Well, you're ugly," Ace replied.

"Don't you want to know *why* you'll never find Starlight?" Faust smirked.

"Whatever floats your boat, evil one," Ace responded.

"With a magic spell, I have taken the stallion *back in time,* where you can't find me," Faust gloated. "I'm going to trade the horse to a powerful, evil wizard named Orgon in exchange for a *dragon.*"

"Orgon?" Ace smirked. "That's a strange name for a wizard. Sounds more like a laundry detergent for gold miners."

Suddenly, a voice boomed out of nowhere. "Your time is up. Please deposit twenty-five riyals to continue your spirit call."

"Farewell, Ace Ventura!" The ghostlike image of Faust began to fade away.

"Wait! Don't go! I was just beginning to enjoy our *kooky* little chat."

But Faust had disappeared. So Ace began examining the area for clues. Sure enough, he found some of Starlight's hairs that Faust had left behind. More important, he also found the trail of oats.

"Come on, Spike, my plucky primate

pal," Ace said wearily. "We must continue on foot. Even though our loyal camel compatriot has left us. Even though we'll sizzle like bacon if we don't find shade. Even though the oat trail leads into that dark, cool . . . cave . . ."

Spike looked up and rubbed his eyes. Dark, cool cave?! Was *that* a mirage, too?

No, it was real! Ace was running toward the cave as fast as his dusty legs could carry him.

"Sanctuary! Salvation!" Ace cried happily. "I sure hope they have cable TV!"

Inside the cave, it was heavenly. Ace and Spike were exhausted. They flopped on the ground. Looking around, Spike could see old bottles, crates, and other junk lying about. Had they been left behind by other travelers?

"Well, Spike, my tagalong mini-Kong, I'm stumped," Ace proclaimed after a bit. "If Faust has really taken Starlight *back in time,* what can we do?"

But they had an even bigger problem. Humphrey had run off with all their supplies — like their flashlights. And it would be dark soon.

"Start collecting firewood, Spike," Ace said, sifting through the junk. "We'll need to build a campfire."

Spike picked up an old metal oil lamp. If it still worked, they wouldn't need to build a fire. He tugged at Ace's pant leg.

"No, Spike. Don't bother me while I'm looking," Ace said.

Spike tried again. He tugged once more. "Oop!"

"Spike! Quit bugging me and find some firewood!" Ace cried impatiently. "Read my lips — fiiiiiiire . . . wooooood. Firewood!"

Spike gave up. He turned and tossed the lamp over his shoulder. It hit Ace on the top of his head. *Clonk!*

"Ow! Hey — is *this* what I think it is?" Ace grabbed the lamp."It is! Look what I found, Spike! It's an old oil lamp! If it still works, we won't need to build a fire!"

Spike crossed his arms. *That's what I said!*

Ace picked up Spike and used him to polish the lamp.

"Oog!" Spike said angrily. He hated when Ace *did* that!

But wait — what was going on here?

Green smoke started to pour from the spout of the lamp. Then suddenly, the smoke formed into a shape — the shape of a genie! It was green and dressed in surfing gear. The genie grinned and grabbed Ace's hand.

"Hey, dude! How ya doin'?" the big genie said. "I'm the genie of the magic lamp! Thank you for freeing me!"

"You're welcome . . . I think." Ace's eyes were going round and round.

"I will grant you three wishes!" The genie smiled.

"Ree-hee-hee-eally?" Ace said dizzily. Then he fainted.

Chapter 5

The heat and the discovery of a genie had gotten to Ace. The pet detective lay passed out on the cave floor. Fortunately, Spike knew the one thing that would wake Ace up. The little monkey stuck his armpit under Ace's nose.

Sniff! Sniff! Ace's eyes shot open wide. "Peeee-yuck! Now I know why you don't have fleas!" He jumped to his feet.

The floating genie was doing some stretches. "Whoa, dude, I've been in that lamp a *long* time," the genie said, touching his toes. "And it's kind of cramped in there!"

"Never mind that, green and mystical," Ace said. "What's this you say about three magic wishes?"

"That's right. Make three wishes and get your heart's desire, yadda, yadda, yadda." The genie grinned.

"Gee-hee-hee, let me think!" Ace pondered. "I suppose I could wish for Starlight to be returned . . ."

The genie made the sound of a game show buzzer. "*Bzzzt!* No way, guy. Can't do it. Can't undo the magic of an evil magician. It's in the Genie Rule Book, section 14, paragraph 8." The genie pulled out a booklet and handed it to Ace.

"I see. That *is* a sticky wicket," Ace said, reading the booklet. "Alrighty then! I wish for you to take us *back in time* to where Starlight is!"

Poof! A cloud of green smoke filled the cave. When the smoke cleared, Ace and Spike were in the same cave, but they *had* gone back in time!

How did they know? The cave was filled with treasure. There were fine silks and carpets stacked up high. Expensive gold vases were stored in the corner.

One more clue proved that they were *really* back in time — they were surrounded by the forty thieves, from the legend of the Arabian Nights! According to the story, the forty thieves were bandits and cutthroats who stole a fortune from wealthy merchants. And they didn't look too happy about a man and his monkey suddenly appearing in their midst.

"Intruders!" yelled the head thief. "Get them!"

"Well, my work is done. Time for a nap." The genie stretched and then returned to his lamp in a puff of green smoke. "Call me when you want another wish, dudes!"

"What are you doing here?" growled the head thief. "Stay away from our riches!"

"Let me handle this, Spike." Ace stepped up to the thieves. That was okay with Spike. These guys looked *really* dangerous.

Ace turned his back to the men and bent over. He used his hands to make his butt cheeks talk.

"Hello. I'm Pete *Posterior*, from the

Butt-er Business Bureau. Somebody reported faulty *gas* lines in their apartment, but I *stink* I've come to the wrong place."

"You're in the wrong place, all right!" barked the head thief. "Torture them until they tell us the truth!" The thieves pulled out big, sharp swords.

Ace whirled around to face the thieves. "Okay, spoilsports," Ace said. "The truth is, we came in search of the wizard Orgon."

"Orgon?! *Eeeeeeeeeeek!*" The big, mean thieves screamed like a bunch of frightened little kids.

"Hmmm. This Orgon must be one scary dude," Ace noted.

"Liar!" growled the head thief. "No one would willingly search out the great and powerful Orgon! Get them!"

The thieves pointed their swords at Ace and Spike. They meant business.

"Suuuuuuuuure!" Ace said. "Let's do everything *you* want to do!"

Chapter 6

The villains closed in. Ace and Spike backed all the way up to the cave wall, onto a stack of carpets.

"We're trapped! We'll have to use another wish," Ace grabbed the lamp. Once again, he used Spike to polish it.

The genie flowed out of the lamp. "Already?" he yawned.

"I wish Spike and I were somewhere else! And hurry!" Ace ducked as a thief swung his sword at him.

Poof! Just in time, Ace and Spike were transported out of the cave and into the desert miles away. The *hot, burning* desert.

"Oop! Ook!" Spike frowned at Ace.

"Sorry, Spike! I had to think fast."

"You have only one wish remaining. And you might want to use it as your ticket home," the genie reminded them, winking. He returned to the lamp.

Ace looked down. "Hey, look, Spike! We

got a lovely parting gift!" They were still standing on the top carpet from the stack in the cave. "We'd better bring it with us. We might be able to trade it for information on this Orgon guy."

They started walking. The trouble was, they didn't know which way to go. Suddenly, Ace stopped. He stuck his nose up into the air. He sniffed.

"I had a dog, and his name was . . . *Bingo!*" Ace smiled and pointed. "I smell oats at three o'clock! Come on, Spike!"

Spike followed Ace across the sand. Sure enough, there was another trail of oats. They followed it for a few hundred feet, but then . . .

Shoosh! The sand gave way under them! Ace and Spike were falling into a pit, oats, carpet, lamp, and all. Someone had covered the mouth of the pit with palm leaves and sand. It was a trap!

Ace got up and dusted himself off. He

looked up. The trap was deep, but not so deep that they couldn't climb out.

"Well, Spike, my familiar fuzzy friend, we really stepped in it," Ace said. "I wonder who put this trap here?"

Spike tugged at Ace's leg. He handed Ace a note he'd found on the pit floor.

Dear Ventura, the note read. *I left this trap for you in case you found a way to go back in time. Good-bye forever!* It was signed, *Your enemy, Faust.*

"Old Faust must be losing his touch, Spike," Ace smirked. "This isn't much of a trap. We'll be out of here in *no* time."

Sssssssss!

That was when Ace and Spike heard them. Four deadly cobra snakes slithered out of the pit's shadows. They were headed right toward Ace and Spike!

"Of course, *no* time might not be *enough* time!" Ace gulped.

Chapter 7

"King cobras, Spike, belonging to the family *Elapidae,*" Ace explained as they nervously backed away from the snakes. "Classified as *Ophilophagus Hannah*, the venom of the king cobra often contains a powerful neurotoxin — a poison that would act on our nervous systems with deadly results. And another thing: Cobras bite when they're angry!"

Spike did *not* like the sound of that!

But Ace had a plan. The cobras might like another sound. The pet detective quickly pulled out his penny whistle. The snakes slithered closer and reared back to bite!

Ace played.

The melody was sweet and soothing. Eureka! It worked! One by one the snakes swayed back and forth. Their eyes closed. They were digging the music!

Ace stopped playing and whispered

to Spike, "Quick, climb out of the pit and go get help!" But as soon as the music stopped, the cobras' eyes shot open and they got angry all over again.

What could Ace do? He started playing again. The snakes returned to their contented rocking. Ace pointed his head toward the top of the pit, telling Spike to escape.

But Spike didn't want to leave Ace. He *wouldn't* leave his pal alone.

"Go, Spike! I *order* you to get out of this pit!" Ace said.

Then a weird thing happened. The carpet they'd gotten from the cave slowly began to rise. Up, up into the air it rose. It was a *flying* carpet! And it was obeying Ace's order! It was taking them out of the pit. Ace and Spike quickly leaped onboard.

As soon as the music stopped, the snakes lunged for Ace and Spike. "Too late, looooooooser snakes!" Ace chortled. He and Spike zoomed out of the pit, leaving the hissing snakes far behind. Soon they were flying high over the desert. Below them was the city of Baghdad. It was a blast! Even the genie came out of his lamp to do a little "windsurfing."

"Hey, I've got an idea!" Ace said suddenly. "Carpet! I order you to take us directly to the wizards Orgon and Faust. Do not pass 'Go,' do not collect two hundred dollars!"

The carpet smiled, changed directions, and immediately shot off.

Ace sat back and rested his head on his hands. "The ooonly way to fly!"

Things were looking up. Except when Spike looked ahead. The carpet was flying them straight into a raging sandstorm!

Before Ace could order the carpet to go around it, they were in the middle of the storm. Sand was everywhere. The wind tossed them about. They couldn't see! Suddenly, a gust of wind blew them right off the carpet.

They were falling . . . falling . . . falling!

Ace woke up in a big pile of hay. How long had he been out? He quickly stood up. He looked around for Spike. He couldn't see his hairy companion anywhere.

What he *did* see was a wondrous sight.

The hay Ace had landed in was on a rolling cart. The cart was part of a big caravan. Several wagons made up the caravan, and each one was pulled by a team of camels. The wagons were filled with all sorts of fabulous things: silks and satins, spices and perfumes, and lots of wonderful foods.

In the middle of the caravan was a wagon bigger than all the others. This wagon had a large tent on it with a sign that read CRAZY AKBAR'S TRAVELING TRADE MARKET — OUR PRICES ARE CRAZY!

Ace jumped out of the hay cart and ran to the tent wagon. He peeked under one of the tent flaps, and he couldn't believe his eyes.

A huge party was going on, and Spike was right in the middle of it, dancing with a bunch of other monkeys! Even the genie was there, hopping to the beat as musicians played.

"Yo yo yo, I'm down with that beat!" The genie danced.

A big, smiling man was talking to Spike. "Crazy Akbar is delighted you fell into my tent!" Obviously, the man was Crazy Akbar. He danced around and jumped up and down like a little kid. He was obviously *crazy*, too.

"Ook whoo whoo!" Spike cheered as he danced with a girl monkey.

"Crazy Akbar's can always use one more monkey!" said Crazy Akbar.

"Oop!" Spike agreed, dancing.

"Wait just a minute!" Ace cried, crawling into the wagon tent. "Spike is my semi-faithful simian assistant! You can't keep him! I need him to help me find Orgon."

Crazy Akbar and the monkeys shrieked, "Orgon?! *Eeeeeeeek!*"

"Crazy Akbar does not like you! You would take my new monkey to the evil wizard! Guards, seize him!"

Two big men grabbed Ace by either arm.

"Take him into the desert and tie him to stakes in the ground!" Crazy Akbar bellowed.

"You don't frighten me, Crazy Akbar!" Ace said defiantly. "I would do anything to keep Spike!"

"The ants will feast on you tonight!" Crazy Akbar decreed.

"Then again, maybe I could let you *borrow* Spike for a while," Ace said meekly as the men dragged him outside.

Chapter 8

The two men roughly carried Ace out of the tent. They jumped off the wagon. Then they let him go.

"So long, pal," said one guard.

"See you later," said the other guard, waving good-bye. The two men turned and ran back toward the tent wagon, which was still rolling merrily along.

"Hold on!" Ace was confused. "Aren't you going to tie me to stakes so the ants can feast on me, like your master ordered?"

"No way," said one guard. "We *never* do stuff like that."

"He's *crazy*! Didn't you notice?" the other guard called.

The two men quickly leaped back onto the tent wagon and disappeared inside. After a moment, Ace ran after the wagon, hoping to find Spike. But it was traveling too fast. He couldn't catch up.

"Well, wash me, wax me, and call me

floored." Ace stopped to catch his breath. He was happy the guards had let him go. But he was heartbroken that Spike was gone.

"Oh, Spike, pint-sized primate pal! How I will miss you!" Tears came to Ace's eyes. "But worry not! Once I solve this case, I will come for you, my friend! Even if I have to search the four corners of the earth! Even if I have to swim the deepest sea. Or climb the highest mountain!"

"Oob." Spike was touched. He was standing right behind Ace.

"Quiet, can't you see I'm emoting?" Ace asked. Then he did a double take. "Spike!"

Spike had followed Ace out of the tent. He'd also managed to bring food, water, and the lamp. Plus, he'd managed to get his paws on something really valuable — a map of the area that included the wizard Orgon's temple.

"*Super* job, Spike, my reliable, hairy

half-pint!" Ace laughed. "Now, let's get to this wizard's temple, get Starlight back, and kick some major evil magician butt!"

The guard at the gate of Orgon's temple didn't usually have much to do. The temple was in the middle of nowhere. They hardly ever had visitors. And if anyone ever tried to attack, he'd have to deal with the wizard's powerful magic spells. So usually, the guard just slept through his watch. But tonight, he was startled out of his sleep by pounding on the gate.

Knock! Knock! Knock!

Wiping the sleep from his eyes, the guard opened the gate. He was surprised to see two nomads standing there. One was tall, skinny, and had a potbelly. The other was short and needed a shave.

"Yeah?" said the guard.

"Hi yo!" said the tall one. "I'm Regis Philbin and this is my assistant, Alex Trebek!"

"Oob," concurred the small, hairy one.

"Your master Orgon has just qualified to win a million dollars! May we see him?"

The guard just wanted to go back to sleep. He was too tired to figure out what was going on. So he let them in.

Once they were safely inside, Ace removed the pack of supplies he'd shoved up his shirt to look like a potbelly. Spike quickly shed his nomad disguise. Soon they were sneaking through the catacombs of the wizard's temple, looking for the stables. Once they'd found Starlight, all they had to do was wish their way back to the future.

But their search brought them to something interesting: the wizard's workshop. Orgon was in there, casting a magic spell.

The wizard Orgon was big and scary-looking, with sharp teeth and a bald head. As Ace and Spike watched, unnoticed, he placed a tiny white mouse on the floor. Then he waved a magic wand over it and shouted some magic words:

"Abracadabra! Give me a dragon as big as a house,
If he eats cheese, he'll again be a mouse!"

Poof! The mouse grew into a huge, fire-breathing dragon!

"Hee-hee-hee! Perfect!" Orgon giggled gleefully to himself. "Stupid old Faust will be fooled into trading me his fine stallion for a mouse. Once the spell is broken, it will be too late! Starlight will be mine! And Faust will be back in the future. Ha-ha-ha!"

"See, Spike?" Ace whispered. "These bad guys even do dirty tricks to each other."

"Ook!" Spike whispered. *Buncha creeps!*

"Of course, it won't matter, because we'll have rescued Starlight by then," Ace said proudly.

"Oob eep," Spike agreed. *Yeah!*

They continued along the corridors. After a while, Ace stopped short. He sniffed. Then he smiled.

"I smell oats, Spike — and that means ⸀ avy!" Ace ran his hands along the wall. "And it's coming from behind this not-so-secret panel." Ace pushed a panel in the wall.

It didn't open.

The floor did.

Ace and Spike fell into a small chamber below. Its walls were lined with sharp, pointed spikes. And they were closing in.

The pet detective and his sometimes loyal simian companion were in big trouble.

"Oob ook ook!" Spike yelled.

"I agree," Ace hollered. "There's too many spikes in here!"

Closer and closer the spiked walls came.

Ace and Spike pushed on the walls between the spikes. But there was no way out!

A spike jabbed Ace's behind. *Poink!*

"Ow!" Ace cried. "I'll never eat shish kebab again!"

Spike knew what had to be done. Without waiting for Ace, Spike rubbed the magic lamp himself. The genie appeared in a plume of green mist.

The genie laughed when he saw the spiked room. "Man! I thought my apartment was cramped! Well, what can I do you for?"

"As you can see, my hairy partner and I are about to make like Swiss cheese," Ace explained rapidly. "So, get us out of here and take us to Starlight."

"You realize, of course, this is your *last* wish?" the genie said.

"That is, unless you want to *lend* us a wish," Ace said hopefully.

"Sorry, guy. The rules are very clear. Section 32, paragraph 1 of the —"

"Genie Rule Book. We know. Just do it."

Poof! — Ace and Spike found themselves exactly where they'd asked to be — in the stable. And there, a few feet away, was Starlight. The genie had granted their last wish. Now he was gone for good.

"Well, I've got some good news and some bad news, Starlight," Ace said, petting the horse's mane. "The good news is, we've come to rescue you. The bad news is, we can't get back home."

Soon Ace and Spike were on horseback, riding the stallion through the dark tunnels toward the big gate. But suddenly, a bright flash lit up the tunnel.

Whoosh! Standing right in front of them were two scary dudes — Faust and Orgon. And they looked *very* angry.

"Not so fast, pet detective!" said Faust.

"You didn't really think you could outwit *two* powerful wizards like us, did you?"

"Welllllll! Aren't you special?" Ace smiled. Then he spurred the stallion on. "Quick, Starlight! Race like your freedom depends on it — because it does!"

Starlight galloped past the two magicians. Ace and Spike held on tight. They raced down several dark corridors. Ace pointed the way. He could smell their way out with his powerful nose.

But when they got to the door, they were in for a big surprise. A dozen guards carrying curved swords blocked the way. But Starlight galloped toward them as fast as he could. Spike closed his eyes.

Then, at the last possible second, Starlight leaped into the air — right over the guards! They were almost free!

"Hooray! Go, team, go!" Ace hollered. "Baba-Ben-Louie was right. Starlight is one fine horse!"

Starlight ran out the gate and into the

desert. Ace turned to shout at the guards. "Looooooosers! Ah-loo, ah-zzzers!"

But their troubles weren't over yet. Faust and Orgon were following them, flying on the dragon!

The dragon took a deep breath. As it exhaled, a fireball rocketed out of its mouth and struck the sand next to Starlight. *Whoosh!*

Starlight, Ace, and Spike zigzagged across the desert. Fireballs hit the ground on either side of them. *Whoosh! Whoosh!*

A pile of boulders stood in front of them. Starlight tried to go around it, but the way was blocked by fireballs.

In desperation, Ace, Spike, and Starlight turned to face the magicians and the dragon.

They were trapped.

The dragon reared back, ready to let one last fireball fly.

In the face of doom, Ace *smiled* at Orgon. "You went through an awful lot of trouble to get Starlight. Why burn him to a crispy critter now?"

"Don't worry, Mr. Ventura," Orgon sneered. "Dragons are very good shots at this range. He'll just get you and your little monkey, too."

Ace stopped smiling. "Ree-hee-heeally?"

Then Ace had an idea. "A *dragon*, you say? Funny, Spike and I saw you cast a spell on this *dragon*. Isn't it *really* just an itsy-bitsy eenie-meenie widdle mouse?"

"What?!" screamed Orgon. "You lie!"

"Why don't you cry about it, baldy?" Ace smirked. He pulled out a piece of cheese that Spike had taken from Crazy Akbar's tent and threw it to the dragon —

the fire-breathing creature eagerly gobbled it down. *Poof!* The spell was broken. The enormous dragon was a little mouse once more.

"How dare you!" Faust shouted at Orgon, enraged.

"That's right, poopy-pants. Orgon was trying to cheat you out of this fine, fine animal." Ace patted Starlight's mane.

Faust shot a magic blast at Orgon. *Zzzzot!*

Orgon fired back at Faust. Soon there were magic blasts firing all over the place. Ace and the animals had to scamper around to avoid being caught in the cross fire.

"We've got to get out of here, Spike!" Ace said as they scrambled around. "It's too dangerous!"

"Oob! Oob eep?" Spike asked sarcastically. *Duh! Ya think?*

Boosh! A magic blast forced Ace, Spike, and Starlight closer to the boulders.

Suddenly, Ace had a brainstorm! "Spike, hand me that magic lamp!"

Spike was confused. *What for? It's no good anymore — we've already used up our wishes.* But he handed Ace the lamp anyway.

Boosh! Boosh! The blasts were getting closer, and they had nowhere to go!

Ace took the lamp and threw it over his shoulder. It clattered onto the boulders.

"Oh dear!" said Ace, "I seem to have *lost* the lamp!"

Then Ace jumped up on the boulder — just missing being hit by a magic blast — and picked up the lamp.

"Oh, here it is!" Ace announced. "I *found* it."

Spike smiled. He knew what Ace was up to now. He jumped on the lamp before Ace even got a chance to use him to rub it.

Once more, the genie appeared in a puff of green smoke.

"You guys again?" asked the genie. "But you've already used up your wishes."

"Yes, but we found the lamp *again*." Ace smiled, pulling out the booklet the genie had given him. "I believe if you consult the Genie Rule Book, you'll find there's no rule against someone finding the lamp *again* and getting three *more* wishes!"

Frowning, the genie thumbed through the booklet. "Hmm. That's not *exactly* correct, but I'll give you partial credit. One wish," the genie said.

Just then, between blasts, the two wizards noticed Ace and Spike talking to the genie.

"Orgon, look! They're trying to get away!" Faust screamed.

"Get them!" Orgon bellowed.

"Return us to the future, to the sheik's palace — stat!" Ace said to the genie. Then he smiled at the wizards. "Loooooo-sers!"

Almost at once, powerful magic blasts

hit where Ace, Spike, and Starlight were standing. But it was too late. They were gone.

Moments later, they reappeared — in the courtyard of Sheik Baba-Ben-Louie's palace! The sheik was so happy to see them, he hugged Ace and lifted him off the ground.

"Mr. Ventura, how can I ever thank you?" Sheik Louie happily patted Starlight. The horse sighed contentedly.

"That's easy — here's my bill." Ace unfurled a huge, rolled-up bill. It was a longer bill than usual. A lot longer. "Returned: one Arabian stallion. Fortunate for you. A *fortune* for us!"

Back at their office in Miami, Ace and Spike sat with their feet up on the desk.

"You know, Mr. Shickadance got pretty mad when we came back from Saudi Arabia and tracked sand all over his apartment building," Ace said.

"Eeep, awwk," Spike replied. *He sure did.*

"And Mr. Shickadance turned three shades of purple when we got those two dozen potted date trees as a gift from Sheik Baba-Ben-Louie," Ace continued.

"Oob oop," said Spike. *That's true.*

"I wonder what he'll do," Ace asked, "when he meets Humphrey?"

Ace closed his eyes to take a snooze. Spike looked at Humphrey standing in the middle of their office, eating corn on the cob. Humphrey smiled. Spike rolled his eyes skyward.

Spike knew *exactly* what Shickadance would say when he saw Humphrey.

"Ventura!"

Who Wants to Be an Animal Expert?

Eyes your mom would die for — Arabian camels like Humphrey have long, luxurious eyelashes to keep out the flying dust. They also have nostrils that they can close during a sandstorm. *Which would come in very handy around Ace's dirty sock pile!*

Talk about horsepower! — Arabian stallions like Starlight are good runners. In fact, most horses are. The fastest racing horse speed ever recorded was 43.26 miles per hour by a four-year-old named Big Rackett. *That four-legged fellow wasn't horsing around!*

World's largest horse — The tallest and heaviest horse ever recorded was named Sampson. He was over seven feet long and weighed 3,360 pounds! *Brings new* *meaning to "riding tall in the saddle," huh?*

Sometimes bad things come in small packages — Even though the king cobra is very poisonous, it's not the *most* poisonous reptile. That record belongs to the golden poison arrow frog of Colombia. Their skin is so toxic, you can't even touch these little guys with your bare hands. Native Colombians use the frog's poison to coat their hunting arrows. *Don't ever touch one of these frogs, or you'll be the one croaking!*

Did you know?

. . . that a group of owls is called a parliament?

. . . that a group of ravens is called a murder?

. . . that a group of kangaroos is called a mob?

. . . that a group of frogs is called an army?

. . . that a group of rhinos is called a crash?